Dewdrop Babies

The Big Storm

Patricia MacCarthy

PICTURE CORGI

It's raining, so the Dewdrop Babies don't need to water their flowers today! Instead, they decide to re-decorate the Great Hall with petals from the garden.

They've gathered petals of every colour:

pink,

red,

orange,

yellow,

blue

and purple.

They glue the petals onto the walls with sticky paste. Bluebell gets into a terrible mess. She has more petals stuck to her than to the wall!

"You don't look like Bluebell any more," laughs Buttercup when she sees her friend covered from head to toe in colourful petals. Bluebell giggles and twirls around.

"I'm a Rainbow Baby!"

Buttercup has an idea . . .

She dips a handful of petals
into the paste pot

and flings them at Poppy!

Now Poppy is a Rainbow Baby too!

Sweetpea and Rose join in the game, and soon there are petals flying all over the Great Hall, like giant multi-coloured snowflakes.

Even Violet can't help laughing when
a shower of petals lands on her head.

The Rainbow Babies dance

and whirl about

until they fall

into a tangled,

sticky heap.

"Oh dear!" says Violet. "We'd better get cleaned up!"

"Let's go outside," suggests Poppy. "The rain will wash the petals off."

"And we can collect some new ones," adds Rose.

They skip through the palace and into the garden.

"Be careful where you tread!" calls a worm. "There are lots of us about. We love rain."

"So do we!" says a snail. "We're going to play some wet-weather games – come and join us!"

The Rainbow Babies join in with the games.

They race with the snails and worms
and play leapfrog with the frogs and toads.

The heavy drops of rain wash away their sticky petals,
turning them back into Dewdrop Babies!

Suddenly a flash of light shoots across the sky,
and a terrible noise explodes all around them.
They huddle together in fright.

"What was that?"

"A m-m-monster!"

"Breathing fire!"

"In here, quickly!" calls Violet. She's
found a safe place for them to hide.

They sit in the dark and keep very still.
They can hear the dragon outside.

Then, out of the darkness, comes a friendly voice.

"Hello there. Wet, isn't it?"

"Who's that?" squeaks Rose.

"It's me, Mole. Who else would it be? This is *my* house!"

"Sorry, Mole," says Violet. "We're hiding from the dragon."

"What dragon?" asks Mole.

"The one that breathes fire and goes BOOM!" whimpers Rose. "Listen!"

"That's not a dragon, that's thunder," chuckles Mole.

"But it's breathing fire," says Poppy.

"Oh dear me, no," says Mole. "That's not fire, that's lightning."

"So there's no fire-breathing dragon?" asks Buttercup.

"No, just lightning and thunder," Mole explains. "That's what happens in a thunder storm. You don't need to be afraid."

He leads the Dewdrop Babies back to the garden.

The storm is clearing as they crawl out of Mole's hole,
and the sun is shining through a drizzle of rain.

"Look at that!"

There,
stretching way up
into the sky above them,
is a beautiful rainbow.

"Now we really are Rainbow Babies!" beams Bluebell.

And they collect enough new rainbow petals . . .

. . . to make a giant rainbow
ceiling in the Great Hall!

For John and my boys,
Laurie and James

THE BIG STORM
A PICTURE CORGI BOOK 978 0 552 55652 1

First published in Great Britain by Picture Corgi,
an imprint of Random House Children's Books
A Random House Group Company

This edition published 2008

1 3 5 7 9 10 8 6 4 2

Text copyright © Random House Children's Books, 2008
Illustrations copyright © Patricia MacCarthy, 2008
Concept © Random House Children's Books and Patricia MacCarthy, 2008
Text by Alison Ritchie
Design by Tracey Cunnell

The right of Patricia MacCarthy to be identified as the illustrator of this work
has been asserted in accordance with the Copyright, Designs and Patents Act 1988.

Picture Corgi Books are published by Random House Children's Books,
61-63 Uxbridge Road, London W5 5SA

www.dewdropbabies.com
www.rbooks.co.uk

Addresses for companies within The Random House Group Limited
can be found at: www.randomhouse.co.uk/offices.htm

THE RANDOM HOUSE GROUP Limited Reg. No. 954009

A CIP catalogue record for this book is available from the British Library.

Printed in China